Where Did Poppy Go?

Where Did Poppy Go?

STORY BY GAIL SILVER

ILLUSTRATED BY AMANDA QUARTEY

PLUM BLOSSOM BOOKS

BERKELEY, CALIFORNIA

PLUM BLOSSOM BOOKS

Plum Blossom Books, the children's imprint of Parallax
Press, publishes books on mindfulness for young people and
the grown-ups in their lives.

Parallax Press
2236B Sixth Street
Berkeley, California 94710
www.parallax.org

Story © 2022 by Gail Silver
Illustrations © 2022 by Amanda Quartey. Licensed exclusively
by The Bright Agency: www.thebrightagency.com.
Cover and interior design by Debbie Berne

ISBN: 978-1-952692-24-6

1 2 3 4 5 / 26 25 24 23 22

Library of Congress Cataloging-in-Publication Data

Names: Silver, Gail, author. | Quartey, Amanda, illustrator.
Title: Where did Poppy go? / story by Gail Silver ; illustrated
   by Amanda Quartey.
Identifiers: LCCN 2022027615 (print) | LCCN 2022027616
   (ebook) | ISBN 9781952692246 (hardback) | ISBN
   9781952692253 (ebook)
Subjects: CYAC: Stories in rhyme. | Loss—Fiction. | Grief—
   Fiction. | LCGFT: Stories in rhyme. | Picture books.
Classification: LCC PZ8.3.S58412 Wh 2022 (print) |
   LCC PZ8.3.S58412 (ebook) | DDC [E]—dc23
LC record available at https://lccn.loc.gov/2022027615
LC ebook record available at https://lccn.loc.gov/2022027616

For my father.
With gratitude to Thich Nhat Hanh

"Papa, where did Poppy go?"

Come along. We'll journey on.
I'll tell you what I know.

Poppy's all around us,
in the soil, grass, and seeds.

He's in the field of flowers

In the songbirds,
and the trees.

He's in the air between us,
in every breath we breathe.

He's in a butterfly that flutters by,

In whirling wind, and falling leaves.

And when you tip your chin upward to the sky,
you'll see him wink "hello."

The light of night and yawn of dawn
are Poppy's after show.

Sometimes he rests up on a cloud,

And visits through the rain.

And when the seasons turn once more, and you ask me yet again, "Papa, where did Poppy go?"

I'll tell you that he's waiting,
in winter's falling snow.

But moments turn to minutes,
and the years will spin you round.

You'll walk upon the soil,
past the flowers in the ground.

You might not see the sky,
with dawn and light abound,

Or think about the clouds,
and the weather they bring down.

And that's okay, because that day,
you'll no longer wonder,

"Where did Poppy go?"

You might miss his laughter, and the scent of his embrace
as you grasp his ever after, in the smile on your face.

But you'll know where to find him.

You'll feel it through and through.

It's where he's been all along,

In everything you do.